DATE DUE

MAR 8 1983			
NOV 22 1985			
APR 1 0 1986			
NOV 2 4 1986			
DEC 5 1986			
JAN 2			
NOV 0 5 1987			
NOV 3 0 1987			

Stanton, Elizabeth
   Sometimes I like to cry

DEMCO

Sometimes I Like to Cry

By *Elizabeth* and *Henry Stanton*
Illustrated by *Richard Leyden*

ALBERT WHITMAN & Company, Chicago

Library of Congress Cataloging in Publication Data
Stanton, Elizabeth.
    Sometimes I like to cry.

    (Concept books)
    SUMMARY: A child recalls different occasions when he
has cried, concluding that there are many appropriate
times for tears.
    [1. Crying—Fiction.   2. Emotions—Fiction]
I. Stanton, Henry B., joint author. II. Leyden,
Richard. III. Title.
Pz7.S79325So   [E]   77-19131
ISBN 0-8075-7537-2

Hello!

My name is Joey, and
I have a big toothy smile.

I also have a very kissy cat
named George.

George likes me to carry
him around.
Then we both smile.

My pet frog's name is
Leap Year.

Leap Year jumps into
my sister Jane's bed.

I laugh and laugh!

My big brother tickles me.
He laughs at me.
I giggle
        and giggle
                and giggle.

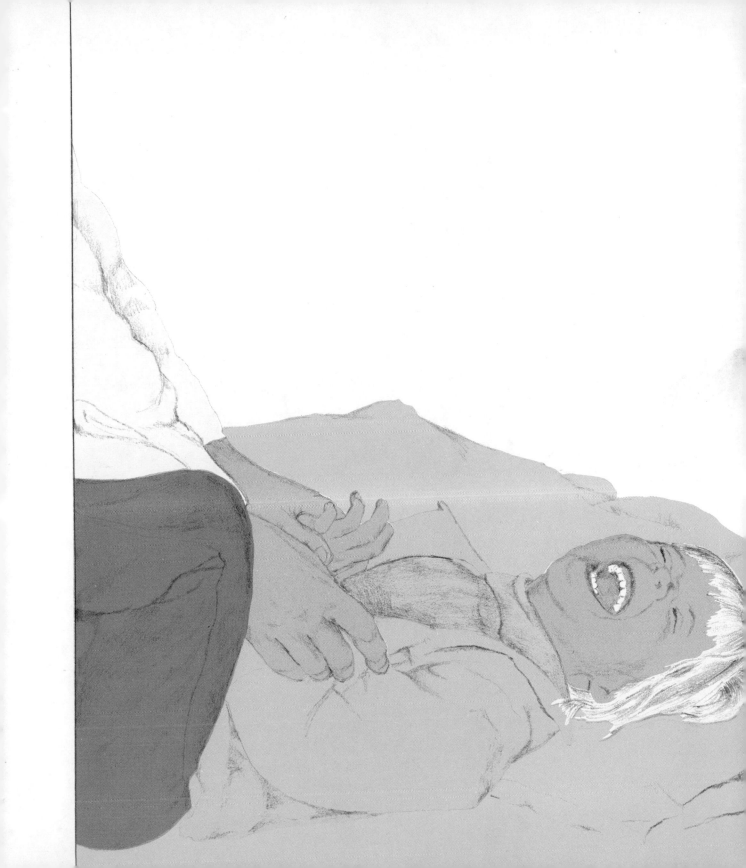

I don't always smile or laugh or
giggle.
I can really scowl when I'm mad.

I *really* scowl at my dog Raggles
when he chews my baseball mitt.

Sometimes I cry.
When I cut my finger,
I cry a little bit.
Then I sniffle a bit.
          I like to sniffle.

I'm not asked to
    Margaret's birthday party,
        and I cry a lot.

I don't stop crying until
my father takes me for
a walk on the beach.

He gives me a ride on
his shoulders, and we
throw sticks for Raggles.

Sometimes when I cry
my sister tells me to stop
being a baby.

That makes me cry even
harder.
Then I get the hiccups.

I drink from the wrong side
of the water glass
my mother holds for me.

I cried when my cat George
ate my hamster.

My mother hugged me and
said it was all right to cry.

She asked me if I remembered
when she cried.
She cried when I ran away
from home and didn't come back
for hours.

I remembered mother crying
when I got home.
I was crying, too, because I'd
been lost in the woods
and I was glad to be home.

Just about everybody cries, I guess.
George cries.
He cries when he wants his dinner.
He says MEEOW,
	but he's really crying.

Raggles cries, too.
He whines when it's cold outside
and he wants to come in.
Whining is sort of crying.
Sometimes at night, he howls.

Today my sister Jane got married.

Everyone laughed and smiled when she and Tom came out of the church.

But during the wedding, when Jane and Tom were standing up there in front, everyone was crying. Even my father.

I guess
sometimes
you cry when
you're happy!